To Annie,
Love from Perfect Peony to
Perfect You!
Bonnie Pryor
March 19, 1991

LITTLE SIMON
Simon & Schuster Building, Rockefeller Center
1230 Avenue of the Americas, New York, New York 10020
Text copyright © 1988 by Bonnie Pryor
Illustrations copyright © 1988 by Jerry Smath
All rights reserved including the right
of reproduction in whole or in part in any form.
LITTLE SIMON and colophon are trademarks
of Simon & Schuster Inc.
Also available in a SIMON AND SCHUSTER
BOOKS FOR YOUNG READERS hardcover edition.
Manufactured in the United States of America

10 9 8 7 6 5 4 3 2 1

ISBN: 0-671-65219-2   ISBN: 0-671-69442-1 (pbk.)

PERFECT PERCY

BY BONNIE PRYOR · ILLUSTRATED BY JERRY SMATH

LITTLE SIMON

Published by Simon & Schuster Inc., New York

$\mathbb{P}$ercy was a perfect grasshopper. Every morning he got
up at exactly eight o'clock without even using an alarm clock.
He scrubbed his antennae until they sparkled. Then he folded
his towel perfectly straight, and made his bed without leaving
a wrinkle.

Percy never complained about going to school. He loved it so much he even went in the summer. He always made straight A's, and he was Student of the Month ten times in a row.

"Why can't you be like Percy," the teachers always asked the other students. Percy smiled modestly. He never bragged.

Now all this would make some parents very happy. But not Percy's mom and dad.

"Relax, Percy," his father said. He was practicing with his rock-and-roll band in the living room.

"Come and have some fun," called his mother. She was doing some high jumps over the couch. She jumped clear to the ceiling, but she landed on the coffee table and broke Percy's favorite trophy. It was the one for perfect penmanship.

"Oh, dear," said his mother. "I was practicing for the Ladies Second Annual High Jump. I am terribly sorry."

"That's all right," sighed Percy. "I'm going to my room to study."

"Don't work too hard," his mother yelled as she jumped over the kitchen table.

The next day when Percy got home from school, he found his father in the kitchen standing on his head. His mother was practicing cheers for the Mayville football team.

"I can't stand it another minute," Percy shouted. He stomped outside and sat on a rock in his front yard.

Just then Dudley Beetle came by on his way to his piano lesson. "My parents are always careless and noisy," Percy told him.

"At my house everyone is perfect," Dudley said smugly.

"I wish I could live at your house," sighed Percy.

"I am sure my parents won't mind when I tell them how perfect you are," said Dudley. "If your parents say it's all right, you may come at four o'clock tomorrow afternoon."

The next day at four on the dot Percy was at the Beetles' front door. All seven Beetle children were doing their homework. It was very quiet. Percy could even hear the tick, tick of the clock.

"This is wonderful," Percy said.

"Shh," said the seven Beetle children.

Mrs. Beetle served dinner at precisely six o'clock. There were carrots and cabbage, brussel sprouts and spinach. "Vegetables every day keep the doctor away," said Mrs. Beetle.

Percy would have enjoyed his dinner if he hadn't been able to smell the sloppy joes his mother was cooking next door. Mrs. Grasshopper made the best sloppy joes in the neighborhood.

After dinner the Beetle family went jogging. "A family that exercises together stays healthy," said Mrs. Beetle.

"Wear your sweaters," said Mr. Beetle, "and don't forget boots and umbrellas."

"But the sun is shining," said Percy.

"Perfect people are always prepared," said Mr. Beetle. "You never know when it might rain."

By the time Percy got back to the Beetles' house his feet were hot and itchy and his arms ached from carrying the umbrella. He couldn't help noticing his parents doing cartwheels in the yard.

Percy wanted to take a bath. But when it was his turn he couldn't find his bubble bath. When he finally found it, someone else was in the tub. Percy went to bed, but he didn't feel sleepy. He missed his mother's bedtime story.

For breakfast the next morning, Mrs. Beetle made oatmeal. It was perfect, without any lumps. But Percy wasn't hungry.

Percy helped wash the dishes. With all seven Beetle children working, the kitchen was soon shiny and neat.

"Busy hands are happy hands," said Mr. Beetle.

"Percy," said Mrs. Beetle. "Dudley was right. You are perfect, just like us. You may stay here forever."

Those were just the words Percy had been waiting to hear, but for some reason he didn't feel happy.

Percy went out in the yard to think.

"Oh me, oh my," cried a baby stinkbug sitting on a rock by the house.

Very politely, Percy covered his nose. "What is the matter?" he asked the baby.

"I was chased by a big ugly toad," sobbed the stinkbug. "Now I am lost, and I don't know what to do."

Percy ran into the house to tell Mr. and Mrs. Beetle.

"A stinkbug," said Mrs. Beetle. "How awful."

"It is a lot of work to be perfect," said Mr. Beetle with a sniff. "We don't have time to worry about creatures like that."

Percy could still hear the baby stinkbug crying. But he knew just what to do. His mother and father would never be too busy to take care of a lost baby, even if it was a stinkbug.

Mr. Grasshopper played his loudest rock-and-roll number. It was so loud that all of the ladies on the high jump team came to the house to see what was the matter.

"This poor baby is lost," said Percy. The ladies jumped in every direction looking for the Stinkbug family.

Mrs. Grasshopper found the Stinkbugs' home herself. She carried the baby home in only five super jumps.

"Oh, Henry," cried Mama Stinkbug. "I've been looking everywhere for you."

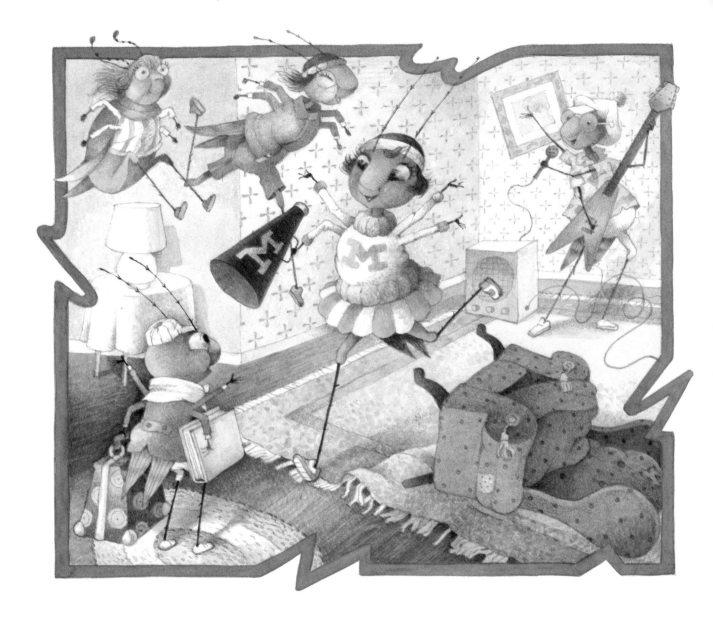

Back at Percy's house, the ladies were practicing high jumps in the hall. In the front room Mr. Grasshopper was singing a rock-and-roll song.

Suddenly Percy knew why he hadn't really been happy at the Beetles' house. He had forgotten about the most perfect thing of all. He had forgotten about love. He gave his mother and father a great big hug.

"Do you know what I like about my home?" shouted Percy. "It is perfect, absolutely perfect."